EA
Crystal Kingdom
Iliana
The Forest
Alhambra
Volcano of the Princess of the Night
Mount Nereid
Kingdom of the Frogs
Lake Garia
Prison of the Blizzard Wizard
RAMION
The Land of Lost Hair

The Land of Lost Hair

Published by

Perronet Press

www.ramion-books.com

A CIP record for this book is available from the British Library

ISBN: 9781909938106

Printed in China by CP Printing Ltd.

Layout by Jennifer Stephens

Tales of Ramion

The Land of Lost Hair

Frank Hinks

Perronet

2018

TALES OF RAMION

THE GARDENER

Lord of Ramion, guardian and protector

THE GUIDE

Friend and servant of the Gardener

SNUGGLE

Dream Lord sent to protect the boys from the witch Griselda

CHIEF TORTOISE

Keeper of the Book of Rules

JULIUS
ALEXANDER
BENJAMIN

Three brothers who long for adventure

THE BOYS' MOTHER

Does not want anyone to see her without any hair

THE BOYS' FATHER

Loves rock and roll, very keen on dancing

GRISELDA THE GRUNCH

A witch who longs to eat the boys

THE DIM DAFT DWARVES

Julioso, Aliano, Benjio, Griselda's guards

BORIS

Griselda's pet skull, strangely fond of her

CLOUD 9

A mischievous cloud, but not all bad

PRINCESS OF THE NIGHT

Lord of Nothingness, source of evil

ALBEE THE ALBATROSS

Spy of the Princess, harbinger of doom

GNARGS

Warrior servants of the Princess

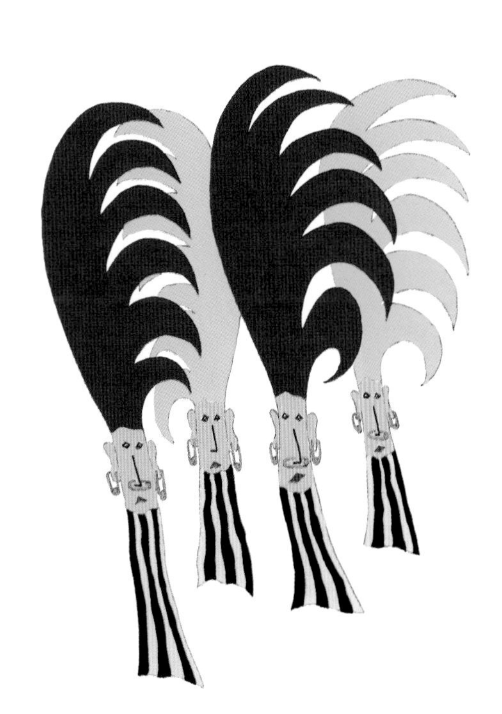

Chapter One

When Snuggle became a legend (Snuggle the Mighty, Snuggle the All-Powerful) many whispered in awe that he was descended from the gods, that in Ancient Egypt men and women had bowed down and worshipped his ancestors. The whispers were almost true, but in Ancient Egypt men and women had bowed down and worshipped not Snuggle's ancestors, but Snuggle himself.

Dream Lord and superhero for thousands of years Snuggle has been sent by the Gardener to protect the lives and dreams of boys and girls (and their parents) from the Princess of the Night (Lord of Nothingness, source of evil). The life of a superhero is often short. When Snuggle fell in battle (fighting against impossible odds) he returned to the Garden, regained his strength, walked with his Master, slept in the sun dreaming of chickens (for like other cats Snuggle was far from perfect) before returning once more to earth. Though born of many parents Snuggle was always the same, was always Snuggle (the name first given to him by an Egyptian Princess). His most recent parents were Belinda and Black Tom.

Black Tom was a scavenger who ran wild in an abandoned granary. Belinda lived next door. She was a most superior cat with long white fur. She had been forbidden by her Master and her Mistress from meeting Black Tom, for he fought, spat and never washed. But one spring day Belinda fell for his careless charm and from their union Snuggle was born.

From the moment of his birth Snuggle was wild. A tiny ball of fur, he shot up and down the legs of Belinda's Mistress, laddering her tights. He jumped on to the table and ate the supper of Belinda's Master. He ran up the curtains, jumped between the pelmets, ran down the curtains and up again and round and round until Belinda caught him by the scruff of the neck, cuffed him soundly and sent him to bed.

That evening Belinda heard her Master and her Mistress whispering. "I'll not have a son of Black Tom in my home," Belinda's Mistress said.

"In the morning I'll drown him in a bucket," hissed her Master.

Belinda lay down beside Snuggle. She felt the warmth of his body. In the morning there would be no more Snuggle – he would be drowned in a bucket. Belinda fell into a troubled sleep and began to dream. She wandered through a garden where plants grew wild and free, roses grew high into the trees, and Precious Plants danced in the breeze.

The Gardener walked towards her. He bowed and smiled: "Take Snuggle to the garage at The Old Vicarage. He has special powers. He has a special job to do."

Belinda awoke. It was getting light and she heard her Master stir upstairs. There was not a moment to lose. She took Snuggle by the scruff of the neck and pushed him through the cat flap. She carried him to The Old Vicarage and they sat in the garden, looking at the house. Then Belinda took Snuggle to the garage and left him alone, curled up in a ball behind the mower. Sadly she ran home.

Later that day the owner of The Old Vicarage went to get the mower from the garage. A small ball of black and white fur shot up his trouser leg, round his back, down his arm and sank claws and tiny teeth into his softly yielding flesh. "Yow! Let go!" he shouted.

The boys' father danced out of the garage, trying to shake the prickly object off his hand. Julius, Alexander and Benjamin looked up from where they were playing. "Daddy! Daddy! It's a kitten! It's a kitten!"

"I know it's a kitten. Get off, you little brute!"

"Daddy! Daddy! Can we keep him? Can we keep him?"

"Keep him! I can't get rid of him!" shouted their father, waving his arm in the air.

The boys' mother heard the shouting and came running. "Darling, what are you doing?" she enquired. The boys' father had picked up a stick and was about to try and knock Snuggle off his hand. "Don't you dare hit him," the boys' mother shouted as their father brought the stick down hard. But she need not have worried: at the last moment Snuggle jumped off into her arms and the boys' father hit himself across the knuckles.

"Mummy! Mummy! Can we keep him?"

The boys' father was dancing, clutching his hand in pain, as their mother replied, "Of course we can!" Then she and the boys took Snuggle inside and gave him milk, leaving the boys' father to nurse his ravaged hand and get on with the mowing.

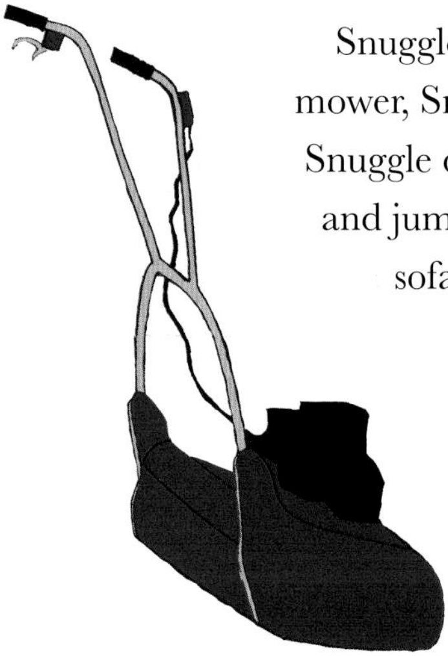

Snuggle was wild. Whenever the boys' father went to get the mower, Snuggle would lie in wait, jump out and try to get him. Snuggle dug up plants in the garden. He climbed up curtains and jumped between them. He sharpened his claws upon the sofa. He ate the children's supper.

"That cat is trouble," groaned the boys' father as he wrapped his hands in an old pullover and cautiously lifted Snuggle from the table.

One day when the boys went for a walk a large black dog followed them home. As soon as the dog saw Snuggle sitting outside the kitchen cleaning his paws, it barked and ran towards him, jaws open, saliva oozing between its teeth. Snuggle showed no concern. Calmly he continued to wash his paws. But at the last moment he reared up and slashed the dog across the nose: the dog ran off howling. The boys went and made a sign which read: "Beware of the Cat".

Snuggle had grown into a warrior cat with great swishing tail, long black and white fur which (when he was cross) stood up on end, making him look huge.

"We ought to change that cat's name to Fang or Attila," grumbled the boys' father.

"We like Snuggle as he is," replied the boys as they looked out of the window and saw Snuggle leaping out from behind a tree and attacking a visitor's dog.

Chapter Two

One evening Snuggle was exploring in the garden when he found a hole where there had not been a hole the day before. Puzzled, he crawled in – and suddenly fell into a void.

Snuggle fell and fell, down and down, through blackness. As he fell he kept his spirits up by singing the ballad of "Cuddles the Conqueror," a warrior cat of old: the noise was dreadful. He landed in a cavern beside a river in a beautiful garden where plants grew wild and free. The Gardener was waiting for him.

"Welcome! Welcome! It is time you learnt that you possess special powers. You have a special job to do. You must protect the boys from the witch Griselda."

The Old Vicarage was a rambling house in a village, low within a valley enclosed by hills. In the hills above the valley lived Griselda the Grunch, a witch who longed to munch the tender flesh of little boys and girls and contented crunch their slender bones. She lived in a ruined tower in a glade deep within the forest. Bats hung from the branches of dead trees; snakes slithered; spiders crept; carrion crows circled in the sky. Along one side of the tower stood a row of cages: they were newly built and standing ready for the fattening up of little girls and boys.

Griselda looked into her crystal ball. She shouted to Boris her pet skull. "Boris! Come here! Look at those three boys playing in the garden of The Old Vicarage. They look very juicy and good to eat. I wonder what their names are." She adjusted her crystal ball and listened intently. She clapped her hands in excitement, and cried out: "The eldest is Julius! The middle one Alexander! The little one Benjamin! They are Susan's children!!! Roast Julius! Stewed Alexander! Benjamin on toast! Just what I always wanted!"

Boris did not approve of Griselda's culinary ambitions, let out a sigh, opened his mouth to protest, but swiftly shut it for he knew that if he said that eating children was wrong the witch would raise her magic staff and send a thunderbolt to echo in his aching brain. Boris was strangely fond of Griselda, although he could not remember why.

When his body was taken by Charlie Stench the Body Collector and his head turned into a floating skull (supposedly with all the powers of evil) Boris lost his memory as well. He could not remember that he and Griselda had been childhood friends, teenage sweethearts, that he had asked her to marry him, to have his children. (she muttered beneath her breath that she would prefer to eat children, not have them!).

Boris knew nothing of the dreadful night when Griselda (drunk on evil spirit) was persuaded by the witch Garesha (who had converted Griselda to the path of evil at the age of three) to phone the Body Collector and arrange for Boris to come and fix his roof (at the time Boris was working as a builder). As Garesha told Griselda, "A witch needs a man like a fish needs a bicycle. A floating skull with all the powers of evil is much more useful!"

Unlike Boris Griselda could remember the night she arranged for the only man who ever loved her to be turned into a floating skull, but she chose to forget, for even Griselda felt a little guilty. After that night she drank evil spirit non-stop for a week. When eventually she sobered up and realised what she had done she sent the parcel containing Boris's skull back to the Body Collector. Then she set off across the universe trying to ease her guilty conscience by doing evil (not with much success) until one night when sitting at a bar in the distant planet of Aralia an intergalactic messenger arrived and handed her a scroll edged in black. Her grandfather Sir Tancred Grunch 7th Baronet and her granny Lady Grunch had died: their nightly quarrel about which of them was the more purely evil had got out of hand and neither had survived the ensuing battle. Griselda was now the Hereditary Keeper of Grunch Castle: her Uncle Peter had been disinherited and sent by Sir Tancred to Australia for doing good, whilst what Sir Tancred did to his elder son David (Griselda's father) was even worse.

On the way back to Grunch Castle to claim her inheritance Griselda passed through a gloomy market. A skull was sitting in a cage in the rain. A sign above the cage read "Boris." The stall keeper was apologetic. "I am sorry. There is a Warranty of Evil signed by Charlie Stench, but the last purchaser (the sorcerer Glob) returned the skull complaining that he would not zap a group of passing peasants with his laser beam eyes, that he did not like hurting people!" To a witch a floating skull who is not evil is an object of disgust, but to her surprise Griselda could not bear to see Boris in the rain. Hardly knowing what she was doing she opened her purse, handed over the money and carried him back to Grunch Castle.

Griselda's guards were three dim daft disgusting dwarves: Julioso, Aliano and Benjio. The similarity between their names and those of the boys was not mere chance. At finishing school in Switzerland (the Berne Academy of Continental Witches) Griselda discovered a spell for capturing the future lives of children of a near relation. Around the same time she also discovered that she had a twin sister called Susan whom the powers of good had adopted at birth to save her from Sir Tancred. "Why her not me? I hate her! I shall use the spell to steal the future lives of her children!"

Many years later after returning to Grunch Castle with Boris Griselda found the spell (her granny had been using it as a marker in a cookery book for roast dragon, stewed unicorn, that sort of thing). She studied the spell with care. She got all the right ingredients from the village shop. But somehow the spell had not gone well. It was a mistake stealing the boys' teenage selves (a time in life when passing from child to adult sometimes the wiring in the brain gets crossed) but out of the range of possible future selves from brilliant to moronic even for teenagers the guards were remarkably dim daft and stupid.

Julioso picked his nose. Aliano made rude sounds. Benjio spat in a repulsive fashion. They scurried around tripping over each other's feet.

"Idiots! Idiots! I said the cauldron, not the cooking pot! Ah, that is better. Now the ingredients: eye of newt, blood of dragon, fang of cobra. What comes next? Ah, yes, slime of maggot." In high good humour Griselda picked up her magic staff. She stirred the cauldron and gave a horrid laugh: "By all that is evil, soon I shall have my supper." She uttered an ancient charm but the boys did not disappear. They did not travel to Griselda.

Griselda screamed, "The spell's gone wrong." She picked up the packet of slime of maggot. It was past its sell-by date. "You stupid dwarves! The ingredients are stale. Who knows what effect that spell will have now?"

SLIME OF MAGGOT

Next morning, when Julius awoke he said, "That's funny. My head feels very cold." He put his hands up to his head. "There's nothing there! My hair's all gone. I'm bald."

He jumped out of bed and looked in the mirror. He did not have a single hair upon his head – it was a dome of shining skin. He ran into the bedroom of his brother Alexander.

"Alexander! Alexander! I've lost my hair."

"Very careless," observed Alexander, waking with a start. Then he put his hands up to his head. "There's nothing there! My hair's all gone. I'm bald too!"

They ran to the bedroom of their brother Benjamin.

"Benje! Benje! We've lost our hair!"

Benjamin woke up and felt his own head. "So have I! I'm as bald as you."

The three brothers ran to their mother and father.

"Daddy! Mummy! Wake up! Wake up!"

"Why are you disturbing us at this hour?" demanded their father. "Go back to bed."

"We haven't any hair."

"Rubbish!"

"Look in the mirror."

Their father looked in the mirror. He screamed, "There's nothing there! My hair's all gone – I'm bald."

Their mother awoke and looked in the mirror too. She let out a piercing shriek, jumped out of bed and hid inside the wardrobe for she did not want anyone to see her without hair.

"Mummy! Come out! Come out!" cried the boys. "We don't mind if you are bald."

"I will not. A mummy without any hair looks very odd."

"None of us has any hair. We won't laugh."

"I'm not coming out – everyone will laugh at me."

The boys got dressed, went out into the garden and thought hard. Then Julius suggested, "We must get Mummy a wig."

"There is a horse in the field," said Alexander. "Let's make a wig from the horse's tail."

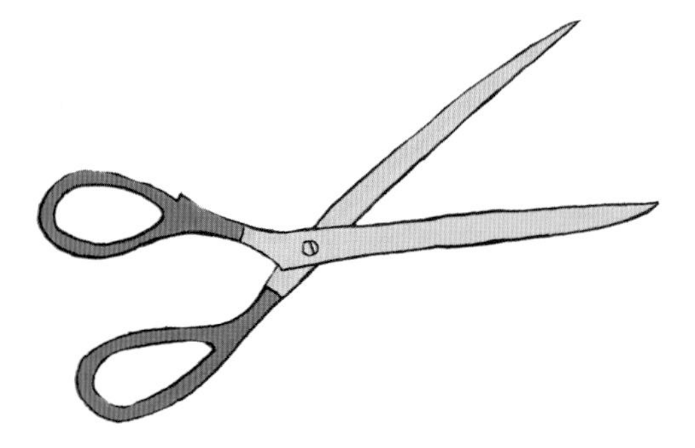

His brothers did not know much about horses, but thought that this was a great idea. Getting scissors from the kitchen they ran up the garden, out into the churchyard, up the path and out into the field. The horse was eating his breakfast, chewing the grass.

Quietly the boys crept behind the horse. Alexander picked up the tail. Julius opened the scissors, but before he could cut the tail the horse reared up, and raising a back leg kicked the boys hard. They sailed through the air and landed in a heap.

"Ow!" "Ouch!" "That hurt!" they cried.

At that moment Snuggle ran up. "It must be Griselda," he cursed.

"But, Snuggle, you can talk!" cried the boys in surprise.

"Of course I can talk," said the cat. "When I get Griselda I shall tear her into little bits."

"Who is Griselda?"

"A witch. She must have cast a spell on you. What we need to do now is to go to the Land of Lost Hair and get back your hair. Join hands, close your eyes and think of your hair."

The boys and Snuggle joined hands. They closed their eyes. The boys thought of their hair as Snuggle gently breathed upon them and they all whirled through the void and landed in a valley.

There was a notice which read, "Private. Keep Out. Land of Lost Hair."

Chapter Three

It was a strange land. All the trees were covered in hair. There were blonde-haired trees, black-haired trees, brown-haired trees and red-haired trees.

In the far distance, well away from the others, stood a group of punk trees with green and pink hair sticking up on end.

SCISSOR
CLOUD SHED
COMB
KEEPER'S HOUSE
HAIR STORE
PRIVATE
KEEP OUT
LAND OF
LOST

Snuggle and the boys paused and listened to strange swishing, snipping, whirring sounds.

"Look over there!" cried Alexander. "Combs! Scissors! Hairdriers!"

"And clouds," added Benjamin.

Combs, scissors, driers and clouds were hard at work giving a copse of trees its monthly haircut. Clouds rinsed the hair, then combs, scissors and driers set to work.

"Darling! Just a little more off the top," called out a tortoise in a pink floppy hat.

Underneath the trees scurried other tortoises with baskets on their backs, collecting the cut hair.

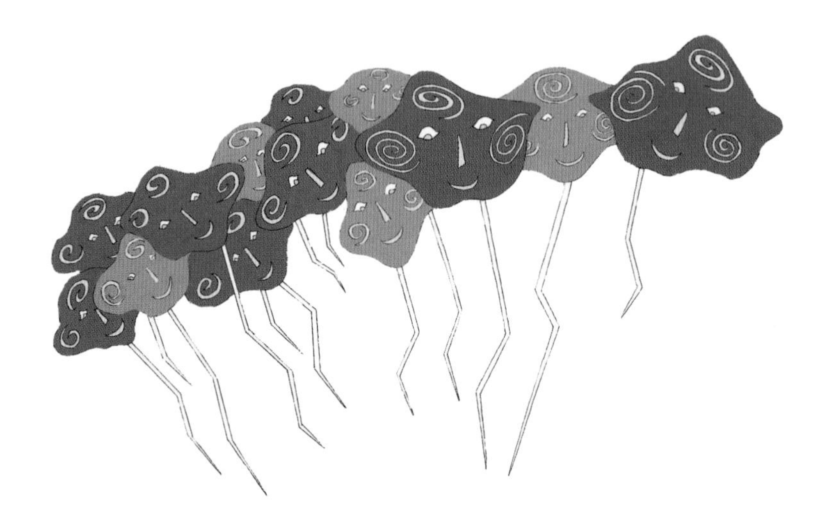

The clouds were not happy. They were tame clouds, captured when young and brought up to obey the rules of the Land of Lost Hair:

Rule 1. Clouds must at all times be clean, bright and cheerful (even when feeling miserable).

Rule 2. Clouds must not spit or make rude noises: thunder and lightning is not allowed.

Rule 3. Clouds must work hard and do as they are told: day-dreaming is forbidden.

Rule 4. Clouds must not wander, whether alone or in company.

And so on and so on…

The Land of Lost Hair was full of rules. At night the clouds had to sleep locked up in the Cloud Shed. As they lay on their bunks they dreamt of wandering lonely as a cloud, making rude rumbling sounds and spitting out forks of lightning.

A hairdrier had nearly finished drying a tree when a little cloud nipped over and with a chuckle gave drier and tree a quick soaking.

The drier spluttered angrily and a loud voice boomed out, "Cloud 9, stop mucking about."

The boys and Snuggle were so engrossed watching combs, scissors, clouds and driers that they did not notice the Chief Tortoise hurrying towards them. He wore a grey top hat and carried a heavy book upon his back.

The Chief Tortoise shouted loudly, "Private! Private! Trespassers keep out!"

"We are very sorry," said the boys politely, "but we have lost our hair."

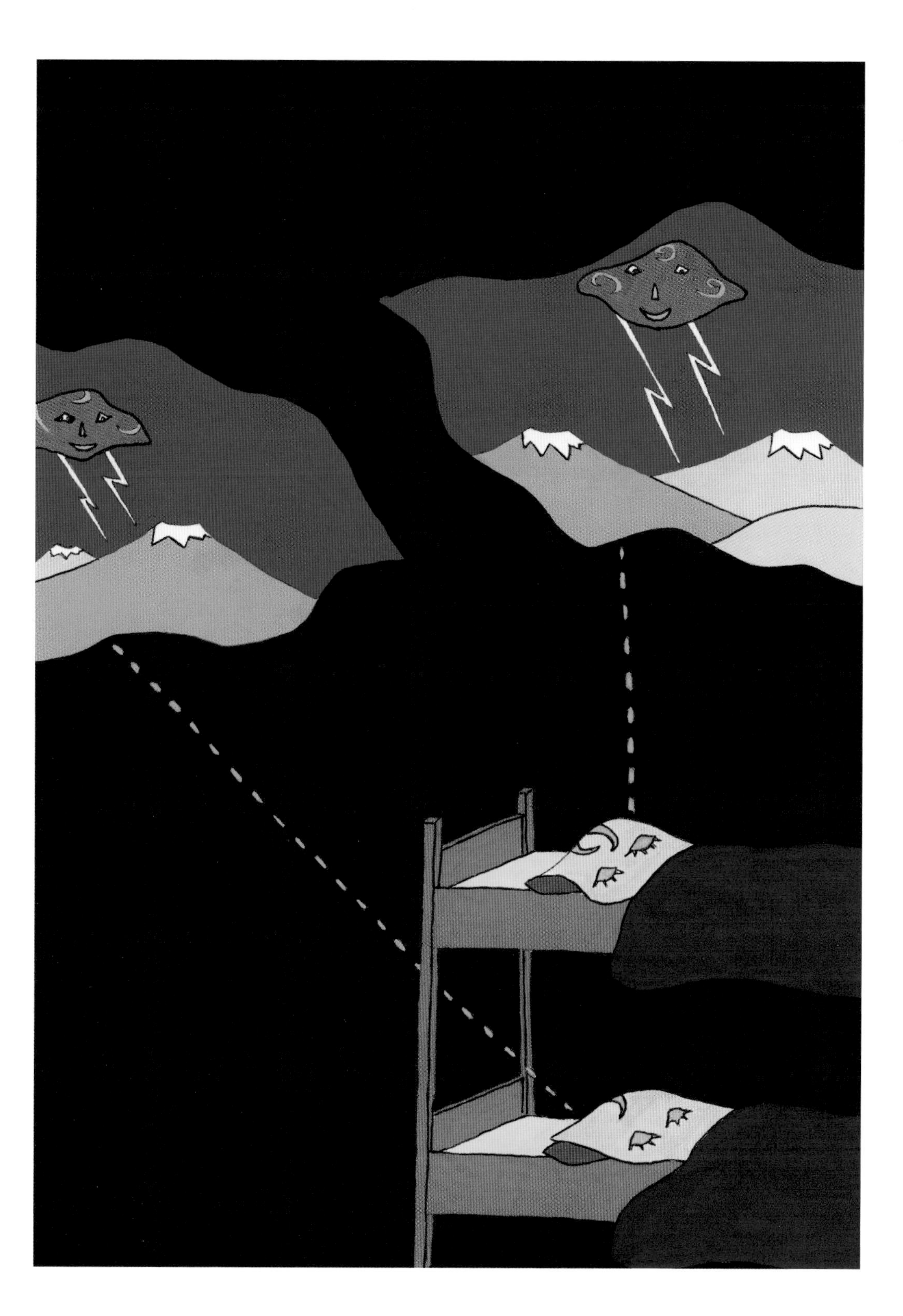

The Tortoise looked serious.

"What are your names?"

"Julius."

"Alexander."

"Benjamin."

The Tortoise took the book off his back and had a look.

"This is very strange. You are not supposed to lose your hair for many years."

"What about our Mum and Dad?"

The Tortoise looked again in his book.

"Your mother should not have lost her hair. Your father should be getting a bit thin on top, but he shouldn't have lost the lot – not yet. This is most irregular. I shall go and find the Keeper."

PRIVATE
KEEP OUT
LAND OF
LOST HAIR

The Keeper of the Land of Lost Hair was a big, black, handsome Slug. He asked the boys and Snuggle what the trouble was.

"We've lost our hair, and so have our Mum and Dad. Our Mum's hiding in the wardrobe and she won't come out."

"I'm not surprised," said the Slug. "You had better have your hair back, but you will have to sign for it. Mr Tortoise – the book."

The boys signed the book. With a whoosh their hair came back.

"What about our Mum and Dad?"

"You can sign for them."

The boys signed the book for their father and, back in The Old Vicarage, with a whoosh most of his hair returned. He patted the thin patch on top. "I wish I had a little more," he sighed, "I used to have such a lot."

Then the boys signed for their mother and with a whoosh her hair came back. She was relieved. "Thank goodness for that," she cried, as she hurried out of the wardrobe and went downstairs for a gin and tonic to calm her shattered nerves.

SCISSOR STORE
CLOUD SHED
KEEPER'S HOUSE

Chapter Four

"We must get home before you are missed," said Snuggle to the boys.

"Not so fast," cried an evil voice just behind their backs. They turned. It was Griselda. Boris was floating on her shoulder and behind her stood her guards. "What nice-looking boys," Griselda drooled, licking her lips. "I'm going to eat you for my tea."

As soon as the Tortoise and the Slug saw the witch they made themselves scarce. The boys began to shake with fear. But not Snuggle: he unsheathed his claws and they glinted in the sun. When the guards glimpsed those claws they fled, while Boris floated to the top of a tree and pretended to be asleep.

"Come back, you cowards!" shouted Griselda, half turning her back towards the cat. Snuggle saw his chance and leapt. He landed on Griselda's head and bit her nose very hard.

"Aaargh!!!" screamed Griselda, raising her hands to her face and dropping her magic staff, which rolled away and disappeared into a huge pile of hair, newly harvested and awaiting collection by the wig-maker.

As Snuggle jumped off Griselda's head, she dived into the pile of hair to find her staff. "Atishoo!" she sneezed, as hair got up her nose.

"Quick," cried Snuggle to the boys, "run!"

The boys and Snuggle ran and ran beneath the trees and had nearly reached the side of the valley when Griselda found her staff.

"Ugh!" Griselda moaned, wiping hair from her mouth and blowing her nose on her sleeve, "I'm going to get those boys and that cat." She pointed her staff at the Comb Store: "Combs, rise; capture those boys – I want them for my tea."

Four huge combs rose into the air, sailed above the trees, then dived. The ground shook as a comb sank into the earth, forming a huge, red fence just in front of the boys.

"Help! Let's get out of here! To the side!" cried the boys, but as they spoke combs sank into the earth behind and on both sides. The boys were trapped.

"Got them! Got them! Boys for tea!" screamed Griselda jubilantly.

But she had reckoned without Snuggle. Swiftly he unsheathed his claws and dug a tunnel beneath the combs.

"Through here!"the cat shouted to the boys. They squeezed through the tunnel, ran to the edge of the valley and began to climb the mountainside.

"No, no, no!" shrieked Griselda in her rage. She pointed her staff at the Scissor Store. "Scissors, snip; scissors, soar; scissors – get those boys!"

Swiftly the scissors flew towards the boys, who by now were part way up the mountainside. Snip, snip, snip, went the scissors. The boys cried out in terror. "Got them! Got them! Got them! Boy kebabs for tea!" screamed Griselda.

But she had reckoned without Snuggle. He ran to a great boulder lying on the mountainside and pushed and pushed. The boulder began to move. Snuggle pushed with all his strength and the boulder bounced down the slope and hit the scissors. The scissors cracked in two.

"Well done, Snuggle!" exclaimed the boys.

"No! No! No!" cried Griselda in a fury. She pointed her staff at the Drier Store. "Drier, rise up; drier, spurt fire; drier – get those boys!"

But at that moment the Chief Tortoise hurried out from behind the Cloud Shed where he had been hiding. He was carrying the Book of Rules.

"This will never do," the Chief Tortoise muttered to himself. "Combs, scissors, and now the drier. They're breaking the rules."

The Chief Tortoise was so cross he forgot all about the fearsome witch. He bellowed at the top of his voice, "Rule 45. Driers shall dry hair and shall be used for nothing else. Drier 36, come here at once!"

The drier heard that voice and flipped. Split between Griselda's magic and the rules, he did a triple somersault and exploded into a thousand bits.

When Griselda saw what the Chief Tortoise had done, she screamed and screamed and screamed. She pointed her magic staff at the Book of Rules and it burst into flame. The Chief Tortoise ran and hid. Griselda waved her staff above her head and pointed it at the Comb Store: combs rose into the air and with a swish, swish, swish, flew towards the boys. She pointed her staff at the Scissor Store and scissors rose into the air and with a snip, snip, snip, flew towards the boys. She pointed her staff at the Drier Store and driers rose into the air and, breathing flame, flew towards the boys. They gasped in terror as combs, scissors and hairdriers flew towards them.

"We've had it!" groaned the boys.

But Griselda had forgotten about the clouds. As the Book of Rules burst into flame, the lock on the Cloud Shed dropped to the ground and the clouds crept out.

Cloud 9 flew to them: "We're free!" he cried. "Follow me." The clouds rose into the sky and as they rose higher and higher they stopped being clean and bright and trying to be cheerful.

"Let's be black and miserable," shouted Cloud 9.

"Great!" replied the other clouds.

CLOUD
SHED
RULE
45

"I feel a rumble coming on," cried Cloud 9.

"Me too! Me too! Let's be really rude."

The clouds all rumbled. Cloud 9 laughed and laughed: "Let's spit out lightning."

Combs, scissors and driers had nearly reached the boys. The boys were in despair and even Snuggle was a little scared. "Got them! Got them! Boys for tea!" cried Griselda.

Snuggle unsheathed his claws. "I can't defeat them all – not by myself," he moaned. But as combs, scissors and driers descended on the boys the clouds all spat at once. Forks of lightning split the sky: lightning hit the combs – they melted; lightning hit the scissors – they broke in two; lightning hit the driers – they exploded.

"What fun!" cried Cloud 9, his stomach rumbling. "Let's have some rain."

"Oh no!" screamed Griselda, rain dripping down her face. "No boys for tea." But one drier had not been destroyed. Spitting flame it flew towards the boys. Then Snuggle leapt. With a single slash of his paw he cut away the safety grill on the side of the drier and, yelling a mighty battle-cry, plunged inside the motor.

"Snuggle, no!" cried the boys in horror as the drier did a somersault and exploded. But they need not have worried: Snuggle sailed through the air and landed on his feet beside the boys. "Are you all right?" they asked.

"A little warm. Let's get out of here."

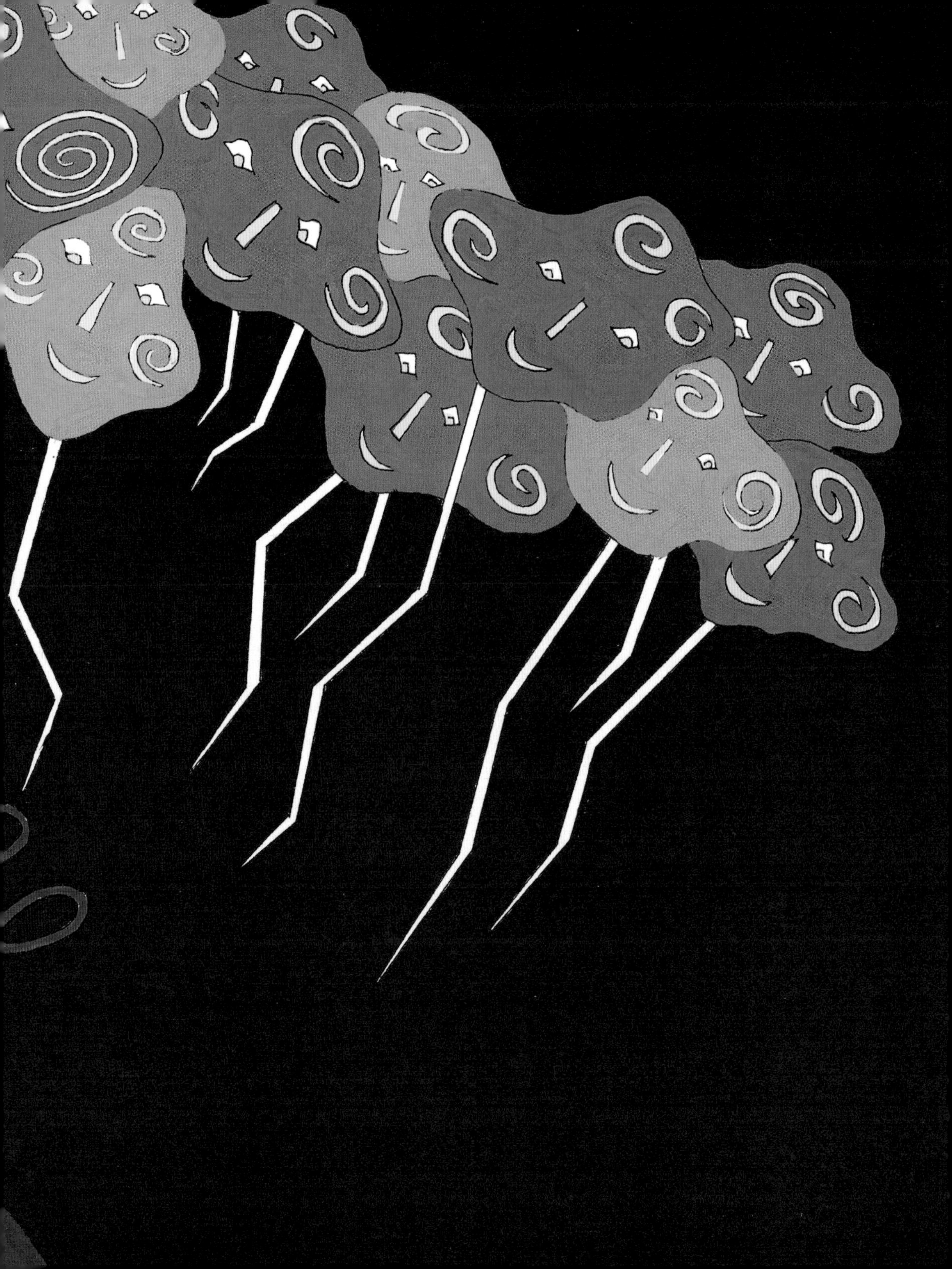

Chapter Five

Down in the valley Griselda ranted and raged. Then a sudden cruel smile passed across her thin, hard face: "On the other side of the mountain there is a high cliff – the boys and cat cannot escape. Come! Follow me," she commanded.

The dwarves and Boris looked at the claw and teeth marks on Griselda's nose and shuddered. "Mistress, Mistress, Snuggle is very fierce. Couldn't we stay here?"

"No!" Griselda screamed, raising her magic staff. "Do you want to be turned into fleas and kept in a circus?" The dwarves did not. Reluctantly they picked up their spears and trudged towards the foot of the mountain. "You too!" Griselda howled at Boris.

Higher up the mountain the boys were still climbing in dark, swirling cloud. They were getting tired. "Hurry! Hurry!" cried Snuggle. "Griselda will be after us."

"I can't go any faster," sighed Benjamin. "I'm only little – I'm tired out."

"Come on, Benjamin," urged his brothers, taking him by the hand. "Hurry! Hurry!"

At long last the boys and cat emerged on to the mountain peak which seemed to be floating upon a sea of cloud. In the distance other peaks of purple heather stood like islands shining in the sun. Then the boys saw the cliff.

"We can't get down there!"

At that moment Griselda, Boris and the dwarves appeared behind the boys and Griselda gave a shriek of triumph: "How nice to see you, boys! I'm going to eat you for my supper."

Snuggle unsheathed his claws and, as they glinted in the sun, Boris and the dwarves shook with fear, while Griselda rubbed her nose. "You won't get me a second time," she snarled. Raising her staff above her head, she muttered a magic curse.

All the cogs and wheels from the exploded hairdriers sprang to life. Whirling round and round, they bounced from rock to rock towards the boys. "Diced boys! Diced boys!" yelled Griselda triumphantly as the boys hugged each other in terror.

Then a strange voice rumbled behind the boys, "Come, fly with me."

It was Cloud 9.

"We can't!" moaned the boys.

"We can," said Snuggle as breathing on them he took Benje by the hand, and led them on to the cloud.

"No!" screamed Griselda, "Wheels! Go and get them!"

But too late. As Cloud 9 darted from the mountainside, cogs and wheels tumbled into the abyss.

Cloud 9 zoomed between the other clouds, down and down, until pulling out of his dive he flew just above the Seas of Ramion.

"This is fun!" rumbled Cloud 9, taking a deep breath and sucking in the ocean.

"Help!" screamed the boys, as fish danced through the cloud and swirled around their heads.

Cloud 9 swooped down over a grim castle on a small rocky island and released the fish over the heads of the guards who had come rushing out to look.

"This cloud is nuts! Completely nuts!" cried the boys in a panic.

"Now look here, cloud," said Snuggle, "it was good of you to rescue us, but put us down, please."

Cloud 9 sighed. "We were just starting to have some fun."

"Put us down."

"Very well. We have nearly reached the Garden."

So saying, Cloud 9 flew over the waves, up across the hills and set the boys and cat down upon a rocky hillside.

"The Garden's down in the valley," said the cloud.

"Why aren't you taking us there?" asked the boys.

"I hate gardening. I might be put to work watering the plants." And Cloud 9 took off, rumbling with deep laughter, and gave the boys and cat a quick soaking.

At that moment a little man in uniform like a railway guard popped out from behind a rock. Snuggle's fur stood up on end and he unsheathed his claws.

The little man was scared and trembling cried, "I am the Guide. I have come to take you to the Gardener. Put away your claws."

Snuggle was suspicious: it might be a trap. He looked this way and that as they followed the little man down the gully to a valley far below where there was a door in a high brick wall.

"Welcome! Welcome!" said the Gardener. "Come and eat and drink. Then you must get home before you are missed."

Blown away by The Land of Lost Hair?
More magic and madness awaits you...

Available Now:

Frankie and the Dancing Furies

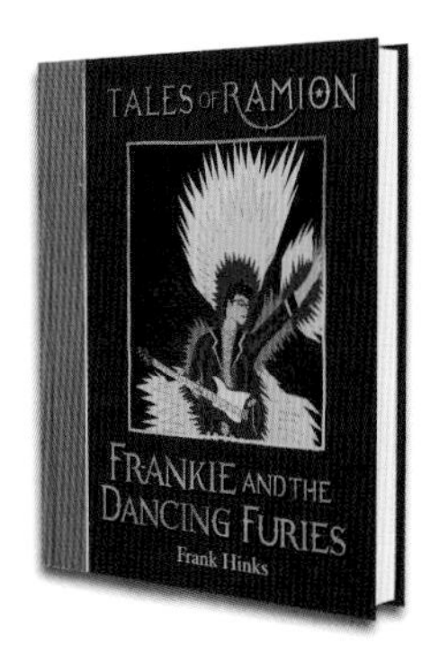

A storm summoned by the witch Griselda (unwitting tool of the Princess of the Night) attacks The Old Vicarage and carries off the boys' father along with Griselda, the skull Boris (whom the Princess wants for her living art collection), the dwarves and the boys' mother as a child. The father's love of rock and roll distorts the spell and all travel to the land of the Dancing Furies where the spirit of the great rock god Jimi (Hendrix) takes possession of the father's body. When he causes flowers to grow in the hair of the Dancing Furies they reveal their true nature as Goddesses of Vengeance.

ISBN: 9781909938083

Creatures of the Forest

In the magical forest there are Globerous Ghosts, Venomous Vampires, Scary Scots and Mystic Mummies, who (like other mummies) cannot stand boys who pick their noses. The boys are in constant danger of being turned into ghostly globs, piles of dust or being exploded by very loud bagpipe music. Thankfully, Ducky Rocky, Racing Racoons and the Hero Hedgehogs are there to help.

ISBN: 9781909938144

The Dream Thief

When the Dream Thief steals their mother's dream of being an artist the boys and their Dream Lord cat, Snuggle, set off to rescue her dream.The party, including their mother as a six-year-old child, passes through the Place of Nightmares (where butterflies with butterfly nets, game birds with shotguns and fish with fishing rods try to get them) and enter the Land of Dreams where with the help of Little Dream and the Hero Dreamhogs they seek the stronghold of the Dream Thief and brave the mighty Gnargs, warrior servants of the Princess of the Night.

ISBN: 9781909938021

And these deluxe collections that include three or four Tales

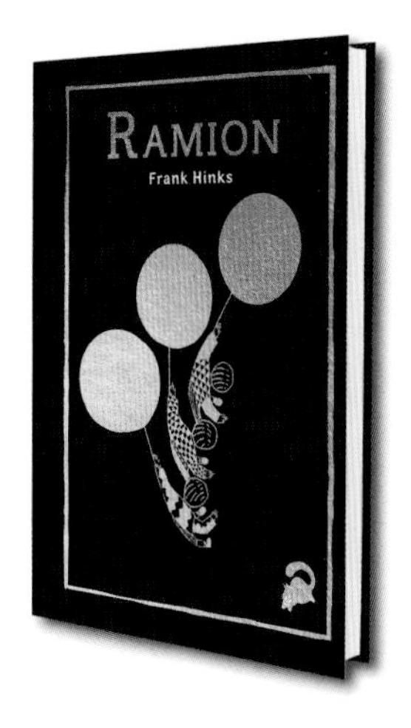

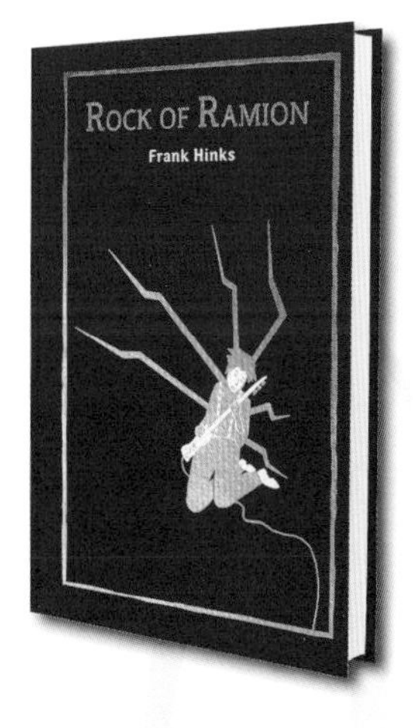

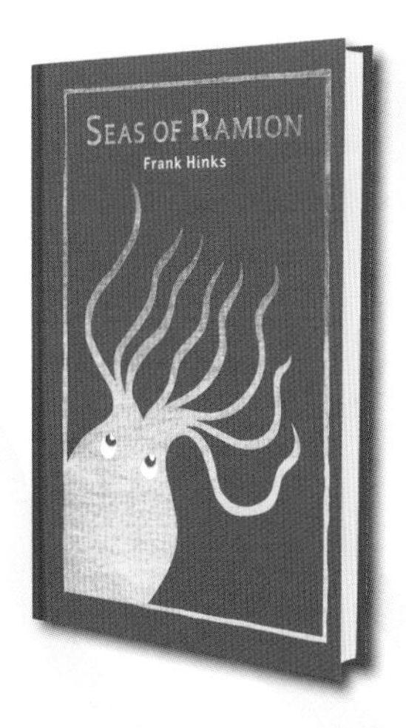

RAMION
ISBN: 9781909938038

ROCK OF RAMION
ISBN: 9781909938045

SEAS OF RAMION
ISBN: 9781909938014

You can explore the magical world of Ramion by visiting the website

www.ramion-books.com

Share Ramion Moments on Facebook

TALES OF RAMION

FACT AND FANTASY

Once upon a time not so long ago there lived in The Old Vicarage, Shoreham, Kent (a village south of London) three boys (Julius, Alexander and Benjamin) with their mother, father and Snuggle, the misnamed family cat who savaged dogs and had a weakness for the vicar's chickens. At birthdays there were magic shows with Scrooey-Looey, a glove puppet with great red mouth who was always rude.

The boys with Snuggle

Julius was a demanding child. Each night he wanted a different story. But he would help his father. "Dad tonight I want a story about the witch Griselda" (who had purple hair like his artist mother) "and the rabbit Scrooey-Looey and it starts like this..." His father then had to take over the story not knowing where it was going (save that the witch was not allowed to eat the children). Out of such stories grew the Tales of Ramion which were enacted with the boys' mother as Griselda and the boys' friends as Griselda's guards, the Dim Daft Dwarves (a role which came naturally to children).

Mill
Lane
High Street
Church
Street
The Old Vicarage
SHOREHAM
Filston Brook
River Darent
Polhill
Arms